DINOFOURS®
Color-Word Storybook
CUBBY BUDDIES

by Steve Metzger
Illustrated by Hans Wilhelm

SCHOLASTIC INC.
New York   Toronto   London   Auckland   Sydney
Mexico City   New Delhi   Hong Kong   Buenos Aires

To Ricky Klausner
— S.M.

Go to www.scholastic.com for Web site information on Scholastic authors and illustrators.

Text copyright © 2001 by Scholastic Inc.
Illustrations copyright © 2001 by Hans Wilhelm, Inc.
All rights reserved. Published by Scholastic Inc.
SCHOLASTIC, DINOFOURS, and associated logos are trademarks and/or registered trademarks of Scholastic Inc.

ISBN 0-439-32046-1

12 11 10 9 8 7 6 5 4 3 2 1   01 02 03 04 05
Printed in the U.S.A.
First Scholastic printing, September 2001

Help Your Child Learn to Read with Dinofours® Color-Word Storybooks

On this page, you'll find a list of several words in color. Point to the first color word (the word "**Danielle**") as you read it to your child. Let your child know that the word "**Danielle**" will be purple every time it appears in this book. Then have your child repeat the word "**Danielle**" back to you. As you read the story, point out each color word to your child.

The first time you read the story, you might want to read it through without using the color-word feature. The second time, you might want to ask your child to read just one of the color words. As your child gains confidence, he or she might want to read a second color word...then a third...then a fourth. It's all up to you and your child!

The color words for this book are:

Danielle	**Joshua**	**Tara**	**Mrs. Dee**
Brendan	**Albert**	**Tracy**	

It was Activity Time in the Dinofours' classroom.

Danielle had just finished constructing a big house with blocks.

"This is the kitchen," she said to herself. "And this is the table where I eat dinner with my mommy and my big sister."

All of a sudden, **Brendan** and **Joshua** appeared with the toy trains and tracks.

"Let's make the longest train track in the whole world," **Brendan** said as he placed his tracks right next to **Danielle's** house.

"Yeah," said **Joshua**. "After we connect all the tracks, I'll build the station."

"You're too close to my house," **Danielle** said.

"No, we're not!" **Brendan** said.

"You have plenty of room," **Joshua** said, putting more tracks down.

"No, I don't!" **Danielle** said. "I'm leaving," she announced. "But don't touch my building."

Danielle stormed over to her cubby and sat down. "I'm very mad," she said out loud. "I'm just going to sit here and not play with anyone."

Meanwhile, in the book corner, **Albert** was just about to pick out his favorite book when **Tara** reached over and took it.

"Hey!" **Albert** said in a loud voice. "I was going to read that book!"

"But I got here first," **Tara** replied.

Albert angrily marched over to his cubby and sat down.

As he sat down, **Albert** noticed **Danielle** sitting nearby.
"What are *you* doing here?" he asked.

"I'm mad at **Brendan** and **Joshua**," **Danielle** said.
"They put their train tracks too close to my house. What are
you doing here?"

"I'm mad at **Tara**," **Albert** said. "She took my favorite
book before I could reach it."

They sat quietly for a few minutes.

Danielle looked inside **Albert's** cubby. "What's that?" she asked.

"That's my toy dump truck," **Albert** said. "Do you want to hold it?"

"Yes," **Danielle** replied.

Albert handed **Danielle** his toy truck.

"It's very nice," **Danielle** said as she made the dumping section of the truck go up and down.

Then **Albert** looked inside **Danielle's** cubby.
"What's that?" he asked, pointing to something in **Danielle's** cubby.

"It's my Princess Dino," **Danielle** replied.

"Can I hold it?" **Albert** asked.

"Sure," **Danielle** said as she handed her Princess Dino to **Albert**. "But don't break it."

"I won't," **Albert** said. He gently moved the arms and legs of Princess Dino. "I like your Princess Dino."

After a few moments of playing, **Danielle** turned to **Albert** and said, "This is fun!"

"Yes," **Albert** said. "We're cubby buddies!"

Then, **Danielle** sang this song:

We are cubby buddies.
This is where we play.
Cubby buddies! Cubby buddies!
Let's stay here all day.

Joshua and **Brendan** heard **Danielle's** song and walked over.

"What's going on here?" **Joshua** asked. "It looks like fun!"

"We're cubby buddies!" **Albert** said.

"Can we be cubby buddies, too?" **Brendan** asked.

"Well, I guess so," **Danielle** said. "Even though you put your train tracks too close to my house."

"What do we have to do?" **Joshua** asked.

"Just sit in your cubby and have fun," **Albert** said.

"Okay!" **Joshua** said. He sat down and began to stomp his feet. "This is fun."

"And I can do my famous growl," **Brendan** said. *"Grrrr!"*

"Now, you're cubby buddies, too!" **Albert** said.

Tracy heard **Joshua's** stomping feet and came over.

"I want to play, too," she said.

"Okay," **Danielle** said. "Just have fun in your cubby and you'll be a cubby buddy."

"I'll sing a song," said Tracy. She sang *Mary Had a Little Lamb*.

Tara looked up from her book and saw her classmates sitting in their cubbies.

She walked over and asked, "Why is everyone here?"

"We're cubby buddies!" Brendan said.

"Can I be a cubby buddy, too?" Tara asked.

"Well, I guess so," Albert said. "Even though you took the book that I wanted. You just have to do something fun in your cubby."

"Reading is fun for me," Tara said as she curled up with her book.

"Let's sing the cubby buddy song!" **Danielle** said.
After they learned the words from **Danielle**, all the children sang:

We are cubby buddies.
This is where we play.
Cubby buddies! Cubby buddies!
Let's stay here all day.

Mrs. Dee had been preparing the children's mid-morning snack. After finishing, she looked around the classroom.

"Where is everyone?" she asked out loud.

"We're here!" the Dinofours called from their cubbies.

"My, my, my," **Mrs. Dee** said as she saw all of the children sitting in a row. "What's happening here?"

"We're cubby buddies!" **Albert** said.

"Yes," **Danielle** said. "We're going to stay here all day."

"Well," **Mrs. Dee** said, "you *could*, but I have your favorite snack today—Dino Crackers!"

Instantly, all the Dinofours stood up and ran to the snack tables.

In between bites of her Dino Crackers, **Danielle** turned to
Albert and said, "It's great being cubby buddies, but eating
Dino Crackers is lots of fun, too!"

Albert agreed, but his mouth was so full of Dino Crackers
that all he could do was give **Danielle** a wide cubby-buddy
smile—and a great, big cubby-buddy hug!